THIS

SWEET PICKLES ®

BOOK BELONGS TO

MARIE

In the world of *Sweet Pickles,* each animal gets into a pickle because of an all too human personality trait.

This book is about Temper Tantrum Turtle who will do almost anything to get her own way.

Books in the Sweet Pickles Series:

Hefter, Richard.
   Turtle throws a tantrum.

   (Sweet Pickles series)
   SUMMARY: Turtle tries every trick in the book to get
her own way.
   [1. Turtles—Fiction] I. Title. II. Series.
PZ7.H3587Tu   [E]   77-16319
ISBN 0-03-042061-X

Copyright © 1978 Euphrosyne, Incorporated

All rights reserved, including the right to reproduce
this book or portions thereof in any form.
Published simultaneously in Canada by Holt, Rinehart
and Winston of Canada, Limited.

SWEET PICKLES is the registered trademark of
Perle/Reinach/Hefter.

Printed in the United States of America

Weekly Reader Books' Edition

Weekly Reader Books presents

TURTLE
THROWS
A TANTRUM

Written and Illustrated by
Richard Hefter
Edited by Ruth Lerner Perle

Holt, Rinehart and Winston · New York

Turtle was walking down the street when she passed
Vulture.

"Good morning, Turtle," said Vulture. "Have you
noticed my new yellow bracelet yet?"

Vulture held up his arm. Turtle looked at the shiny yellow bracelet. "That's neat," she said. "Let me try it on."

"No," said Vulture. "It's my bracelet and it looks better on me than anybody else, and you can't try it on."

"But I want to try it," whined Turtle. "I want it on."
"You can't have it," grumbled Vulture. "It's mine."

Turtle sniffled and moaned, "I don't care! I want it.
I want it now!"
"No!" yelled Vulture.

Turtle rolled her eyes and said, "You better give it
to me. You better give it to me right now!"
"What if I don't?" shouted Vulture.

"Then I'll scream," said Turtle. She threw back her head and screamed at the top of her lungs. "YAAAHHH! YAAAHHHHHHH! I want it!"

Walrus came running over.
"What's the matter?" he asked. "Who is making that terrible noise?"

"YAAAAAAAAAHHHHHHHHH!" screamed Turtle.
"It's only Turtle," sneered Vulture. "She wants my
bracelet and I won't give it to her."

Walrus looked at Turtle. "Listen to me," he said.
"That bracelet belongs to Vulture and he doesn't
have to give it to you if he doesn't want to."

"But I WAAANT IT!" screeched Turtle. "MAKE HIM GIVE IT TO MEEEEEE. YAAAAAHHHHH!"

Lion came running over.

"What's the matter with Turtle?" he asked.

"She wants Vulture's bracelet," moaned Walrus.

"And I won't give it to her," yelled Vulture.

"GIVE IT TO ME!" screamed Turtle,
"OR I'LL KICK AND SCREAM AND STAMP
MY FEET! YAAAAAAAHHHHHHHH!"

"No," said Vulture.

Turtle kicked and screamed and stamped her feet.

"Oh, dear," sighed Lion. "Maybe you ought to give her the bracelet."

"YESSSSSSS," screamed Turtle. "GIVE IT TO MEEE!"

"No," said Vulture. "I won't. It's mine."

"This could get to be a problem," moaned Walrus.

"EEEEOOOOWWWWW," screamed Turtle. "YAAAOOOWWW!"

Yak and Zebra came by.

"What's this all about?" asked Yak. "Turtle seems to be screaming."

"And kicking and stamping her feet," smiled Zebra.

"She wants my bracelet," grumbled Vulture, "and I won't give it to her."

"MAKE HIM GIVE IT TO ME!" screamed Turtle, "OR I'LL KICK AND SCREAM AND STAMP MY FEET AND THROW MYSELF ON THE GROUND." Turtle kicked and screamed and stamped her feet and threw herself on the ground.

"This is really serious," groaned Walrus.

"WAAHHHHHHH. EEOOOWWWWWW. YARRRGH!" screamed Turtle.

Hippo jogged over. "What's the matter?" he cried. "Is somebody hurt?"

"YEEEEOOOW!" screeched Turtle.

"I WANT IT. WAAAHHH!"

"What can we do for her?" asked Lion.

"How can we make her stop?" moaned Walrus.

"What's going on?" asked Camel as she passed by. "Turtle wants something," said Hippo. "I'm not sure what it is, but she said she would kick and scream and stamp her feet and throw herself on the ground until she gets it."

"YOU BETTER GIVE IT TO ME," screamed Turtle,
"OR I'LL HOLD MY BREATH UNTIL I TURN BLUE!"
Everybody looked at Turtle.
Turtle took a deep breath and puffed out her cheeks.

"This *is* a problem," groaned Walrus. "She could hurt herself."
Turtle stamped her feet and threw herself on the ground.

"I think I can make her stop," said Zebra.
Turtle kicked and thumped and started to turn blue.
"Come on over here, everybody!" called Zebra.
Turtle jumped up and down and waved her arms and kept on turning blue.

Zebra started whispering.

"If we all kick and scream and stamp our feet and yell and hold our breath," smiled Zebra, "Turtle will see how silly it looks."

They all started to scream.

"OOOOOOWAAAAHHHH!" wailed Walrus.
"GIVE IT TO ME!"

"OOOH, OOOH, OOOH!" screeched Lion. "I WANT IT!"

"YAARGH. YEEEOOOWW. AAARGH!" yelled Yak.
"MINE! MINE!"

Zebra screamed and jumped up and down and stood on his head and kicked his feet.

Hippo yelled and moaned and cried and sniffled and rolled into Turtle.

Turtle looked up.

Yak drummed his feet and held his breath.
Camel cried and wailed and groaned and jumped up and down.
Zebra pounded on the ground and screeched.
Walrus rolled over and over and over.

"YEEEEOOOOWW!" they all screamed.
"GIVE IT TO MEEEE!"
Turtle let out her breath with a WHOOSH.

"AAAARRRRGGHH!" screeched everyone.
"ME! ME! IT'S MINE!"
Turtle stopped kicking and stamping.

"GIVE IT TO MEEEE!" shouted everyone.
Hippo banged his head with his hand.
Zebra cried and shuffled.
Yak hiccuped and held his breath.
Lion crossed his eyes and bit his tail.

Turtle walked over to Vulture.

"Hey, Vulture," she said. "What are all those guys doing?"

"I think they all want my bracelet," grumbled Vulture.

"Well," said Turtle. "I wouldn't give it to them if I were you."
Turtle walked off down the street.

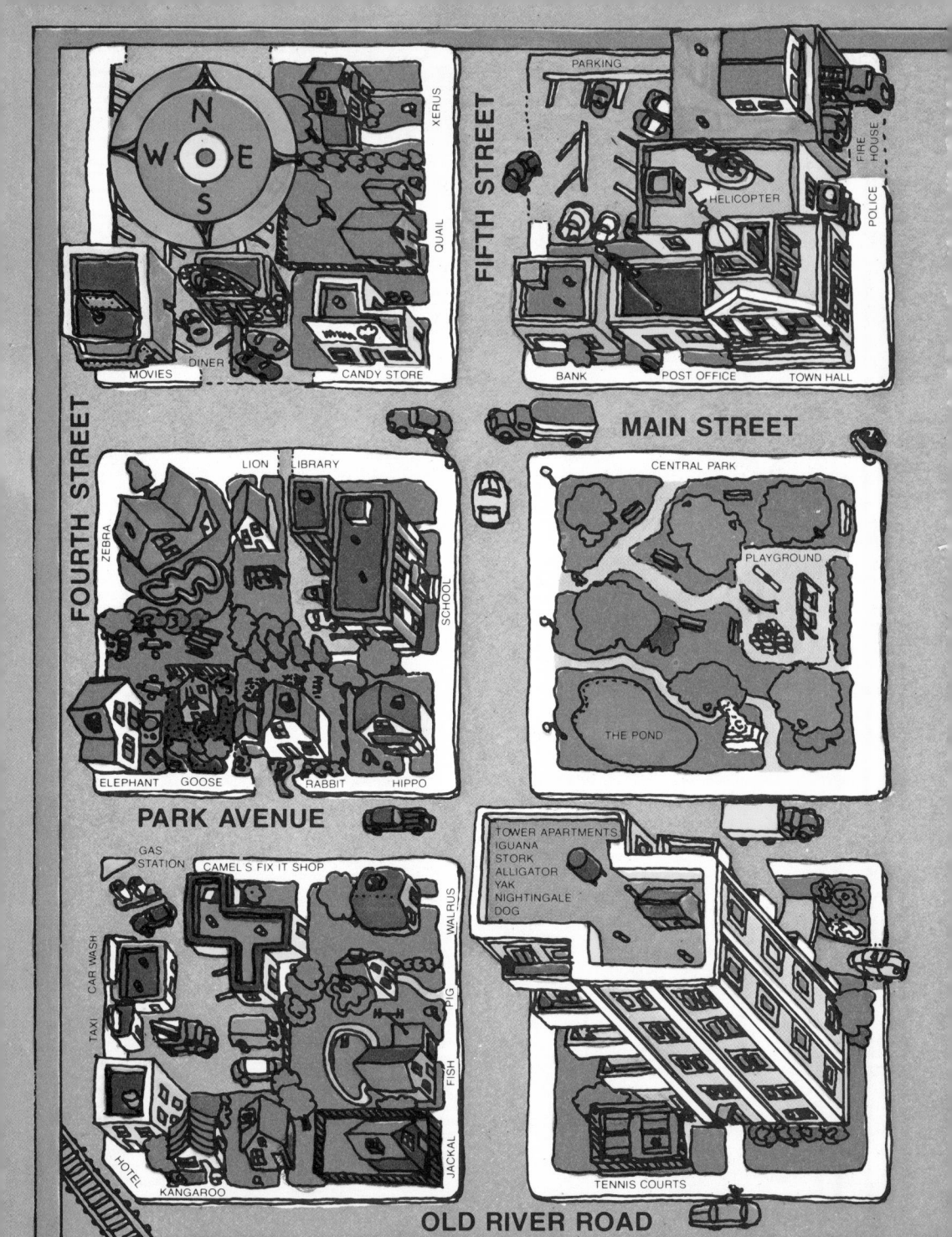